HANS CHRISTIAN ANDERSEN

HANS CLODHOPPER

HANS CHRISTIAN ANDERSEN

HANS

J. B. LIPPINCOTT COMPANY

CLODHOPPER

RETOLD & ILLUSTRATED
BY LEON SHTAINMETS

PHILADELPHIA · NEW YORK

U.S. Library of Congress Cataloging in Publication Data
Shtainmets, Leon.
Hans Clodhopper.
SUMMARY: With a dead crow, a damaged wooden shoe, and mud from the side of the road, Hans
convinces the princess that he is clever enough to marry her.
[1. Fairy tales] I. Andersen, Hans Christian, 1805-1875. Klods-Hans. II. Title.
PZ8.S34514Han   [E]   74-23674   ISBN-0-397-31614-3

Once there was a Princess who announced far and wide that she would soon choose a husband. *Only the Clever Need Apply*, the announcement said, for the Princess would marry none but the man who had an answer to everything. Out in the country, in an old manor house, lived an old Squire with his three sons. Two of the sons, who were twice as clever as anyone needs to be, made up their minds to propose to the Princess.

The brothers spent a week getting ready. It was all the time they had, but they felt it was quite enough, since they already knew so much.

One brother knew the whole Latin dictionary by heart, and he could recite from beginning to end or from end to beginning everything that had appeared in the city newspapers for three years.

The other brother had memorized all the village laws, so he felt competent to talk about affairs of state. Besides that, he knew how to embroider suspenders, and had a lot to say on that subject.

"I shall win the King's daughter," they each said.

On the day the brothers were to leave for the royal court, their father gave them each a beautiful horse. The one who could repeat the dictionary and the newspapers got a coal black horse, while the one who knew all about village laws and embroidery got a milk white horse. Then the brothers smeared the corners of their mouths with oil, to make the words slide out faster.

All the servants were gathered in the courtyard to see them off, when along came the third brother. No one paid much attention to this brother. He was called Hans Clodhopper because everyone thought the things he did were silly at best and foolish at worst. Strange to say, Hans Clodhopper seemed to like the way he was.

"Where are you going, dressed up in your best clothes?" Hans asked his clever brothers.

"We're going to the royal court, to talk our way into the Princess's good graces. How come you haven't heard? Every town crier is shouting about it, all over the land. The Princess will marry the man who has an answer to everything."

"What news!" said Hans Clodhopper. "I'm coming too."

The clever brothers laughed. "How could a clodhopper like you have an answer to anything?" they asked, and rode away.

"Father, let me have a horse!" cried Hans Clodhopper. "Suddenly I feel like getting married to the Princess. If she'll marry me, fine. If not, I'll marry her!"

"Stuff and nonsense!" said the Squire. "You'll get no horse from me. What would you have to say to a Princess? Your brothers are a different matter; fine clever fellows, they are."

"Well, if you won't give me a horse," said Hans Clodhopper, "I'll take my goat. He's my own, and he'll get me there."

   With that he seated himself on his billy goat, dug his heels into its sides, and galloped off down the road as fast as lightning.

   "Out of my way!" shouted Hans Clodhopper, and sang at the top of his lungs.

The two clever brothers were riding on ahead, not saying a word. They had to think about everything they knew and carefully rehearse witty speeches.

"Hey, there," shouted Hans Clodhopper to his brothers. "Here I come! Look what I found on the road!" He held up a dead crow for his brothers to see.

"You clodhopper!" they said. "What on earth is that for?"

"I'll give it to the King's daughter."

"You just try it!" They laughed and kept on riding.

"Hey, wait!" Hans shouted again. "Look what else I found! You don't come across stuff like this on the road every day."

The brothers turned around to see what it was. "What a clodhopper," they said. "It's just an old wooden shoe with the top part missing. Is that for the Princess, too?"

"By all means," answered Hans Clodhopper.

The brothers laughed and rode on.

"Aha!" Hans shouted again. "It's getting better and better. Just look at this! Ha! It's perfect."

"What have you got this time?" asked the brothers.

"I won't tell you, no, sir. But the Princess will be delighted!"

"Ugh," said the brothers. "It's only mud from the ditch."

"Exactly," said Hans Clodhopper. "Such fine mud that I can't even hold it—it runs between my fingers." And he filled his pocket with the mud.

The brothers rode on ahead and arrived an hour before Hans. They stopped at the city gates, where all the suitors, who had come from far and wide, were given numbers in order of their arrival. The suitors were arranged in rows so close together that they couldn't even move their arms. This was a good thing, since otherwise they would have pushed and shoved at each other just to get to the front.

Hundreds of people crowded around the castle and peeped in the windows, hoping to see whom the Princess would choose. One by one the suitors were ushered into the hall, and one by one they were ushered out.

At last came the turn of the brother who knew the dictionary and newspapers by heart. The floor of the great hall creaked under his feet, and the ceiling was covered with mirrors, so that he saw himself standing on his head. This made him very nervous. To make matters worse, there was the City Councilman with his clerks, waiting to write down every word that was said, so the story could be sent to the newspapers and sold on street corners for a penny.

To top it off, the stove in the room was going full blast, so that its pipe was red-hot. *I must say something clever,* the brother thought, but suddenly he was tongue-tied.

"It's awfully hot in here," he said at last, and the clerks quickly wrote it down.

"That's because my father is roasting chickens today," answered the Princess.

"Uh, huh," was all he could think to say. He certainly hadn't expected a conversation like this. He searched his brain for something witty to say, but there hadn't been anything in the Latin dictionary or the newspapers about roasting chickens.

"Uh, huh," he said again.

"No good!" declared the Princess. "Out!" And he had to leave.

The second brother walked in.
"It's terribly hot in here," he said.
"Yes, we're roasting chickens," said the Princess.
"What did — what?" he asked.
All the clerks wrote down: "What did — what."
"No good!" said the Princess. "Out!"

And then Hans Clodhopper rode into the hall on his billy goat.

"Wow, it's hot enough in here to cook something!" he said.

"That's because I'm roasting chickens," said the Princess.

"That is very convenient," said Hans Clodhopper. "Do you suppose I can get this crow roasted?"

"Of course," said the Princess. "But what will you roast it in? I don't have a pot or pan."

"But I have," said Hans Clodhopper. "This will make a pot." And he pulled out the old wooden shoe and put the crow in it.

"That's enough for a whole meal," said the Princess. "And where will you get the drippings to baste it with?"

"I have some here," answered Hans Clodhopper, and he took some mud out of his pocket. "Take it, there's plenty."

"Now that's what I like!" exclaimed the Princess. "A man who has an answer to everything. For that I'm going to marry you. But do you realize that the Councilman is writing down everything we say for the newspapers? You know, the Councilman can be a little dangerous. Some say he twists the truth to make fools of people. Others say he's lived longer than his brains. Either way, he never gets anything right."

She said this to see if she could fluster Hans, but the Councilman's clerks whooped with delight and spattered the floor with ink.

"Ah, so he's the big shot," said Hans Clodhopper. "In that case, I must give him something special." And he emptied his pockets and threw the mud in the Councilman's face.

"Terrific!" cried the Princess. "I would never have thought of that myself. But with you by my side I'll soon learn!"

That is how Hans Clodhopper became the King and was given both a wife and a crown. We read about this in the story written by the Councilman. So, of course, we know it's true.

HANS CHRISTIAN ANDERSEN was born in 1805 in the old Danish city of Odense. Over the door of the one-room house where he spent his childhood hung a wooden sign bearing a two-headed eagle. This was not a royal coat of arms; Hans' father was a shoemaker, and the double-headed eagle signified only that shoes come in pairs.

In this northern fog-shrouded city there was little that was beautiful or bright, and the Andersens' poor home was drabber than most. But Hans was a born storyteller and for him the world was enchanted. The creaking of the rafters and the voice of the wind in the chimney told him tales. On the stage of the toy theater he had built he enacted dramas with puppets he had made himself. And in the streets he told his stories to passersby, who listened to him spellbound.

Success did not come as easily to Hans Christian Andersen as it had to his puppet heroes. He said that, like a mountaineer who carves out footholds in a granite cliff, he won his place in literature slowly and with great difficulty. His keen eye for the pretentious and his willingness to prick the balloon of overblown self-importance gained him enemies among the powerful and influential. He often found himself opposed by critics and the press. But the magic of his stories—which he wrote quickly, as though fearing that the fantasies might disappear before he could get them down—was stronger than the disapproval of his enemies. A nutshell became a boat for tiny Thumbelina, the ugly duckling grew to be a swan, and the little tin soldier was not a worn-out toy but a brave, strong person. In the end kings considered it an honor to shake Andersen's hand.

Hans Christian Andersen died in 1875. His fame has spread far beyond the borders of Denmark. He was indeed a magician. Today people everywhere know his name from childhood—and one need only utter it to bring to life a whole fairy-tale world, inhabited by touching, funny, sad, and merry beings whose fate is always extraordinary.

To the memory of Hans Christian Andersen, the artist and publisher dedicate this book.

LEON SHTAINMETS graduated from the Moscow Academy of Arts School in 1963 and was accepted as a Member of the Union of Artists of the USSR in 1970. A citizen of the USSR, he has lived in several European countries and now makes his home in Philadelphia with his wife and son. His work has been exhibited in Austria, Finland, Spain, and the USSR, and he has held one-man shows in Moscow and Rome. His paintings, drawings, and lithographs can be found in museums, galleries, and private collections in Moscow, London, Rome, Madrid, New York, and Philadelphia. He has illustrated more than twenty books for children and adults. HANS CLODHOPPER is the first of these to be published in the United States.